The Sloth Who Slowed Us Down

By **Margaret Wild**

Illustrated by **Vivienne To**

Abrams Books for Young Readers
New York

For Jack

— Margaret

For Phil, Yve, and my niece

— Vivienne

Cataloging-in-Publication Data has been applied for and may be obtained
from the Library of Congress.

ISBN 978-1-4197-3195-2

Book design by Mercedes Padró

2017 © Text, Margaret Wild; 2017 © Illustrations, Vivienne To.
First published 2017 in the English language by Allen & Unwin, Sydney,
Australia. Published in 2018 by Abrams Books for Young Readers, an
imprint of ABRAMS. All rights reserved. No portion of this book may be
reproduced, stored in a retrieval system, or transmitted in any form or by
any means, mechanical, electronic, photocopying, recording, or otherwise,
without written permission from the publisher.

Printed and bound in China
10 9 8 7 6 5 4 3 2 1

Abrams Books for Young Readers are available at special discounts when
purchased in quantity for premiums and promotions as well as fundraising
or educational use. Special editions can also be created to specification.
For details, contact specialsales@abramsbooks.com or the address below.

ABRAMS The Art of Books
195 Broadway, New York, NY 10007
abramsbooks.com

Amy's family was the speediest family in the world.

They walked fast,

drove fast,

shopped fast,

and ate fast.

There was never any time to talk or play or laugh or laze . . .

. . . until the afternoon Amy brought a sloth home to stay. "Where on earth did you find him?" Dad asked.

"Hanging from a tree in the park," Amy said, plucking one beetle and two moths from his fur.

Mom shuddered. "He needs a bath," she said.

Sloth shook his head very, very slowly, because sloths do everything slowly. "Right away," said Mom.

"I have to warn you, Sloth," Amy whispered. "We are the fastest family in the entire world."

Sloth had a long, leisurely bath with lots of bubbles, a purple duck, and a red boat.

He dried himself slowly,

combed his fur slowly,

admired himself for ages in the mirror, and
then crawled down the stairs for dinner.

INSTANT MEALS

5 MINUTE MEALS

15 MINUTE MEALS

20 MINUTE MEALS

THINK FASTER

Amy, Mom, and Dad were already sitting at the table.

"Hurry up, buddy," said Dad.

"Chop-chop," said Mom.

"See what I mean, Sloth?" Amy said with a sigh.

Sloth ate very, very slowly.

He was so slow that Amy had plenty of time to talk about the things that had happened that day.

"How amazing!" said Mom.

"I wish I'd been there!" said Dad.

When Sloth had finished helping
(very slowly) to do the dishes, Dad said,
"There's just enough time for a quick trot
around the block before bedtime."

But Sloth couldn't trot.

He dragged himself along,

very, very slowly.

So slowly that Amy and Mom and Dad had plenty of time to chat with the neighbors,

pet a cat,

throw a stick for a friendly dog,

admire the moon, and try to find the red star.

When they got home, Sloth made himself comfortable hanging from a tree in the garden. Amy hugged him good night.

"Thank you," she whispered.
"This has been the best day of my life."

1001 TYPES of MOSS

Sloth stayed for three glorious weeks.

But one morning, Sloth moved next door . . .

. . . to the new speediest family in the world.

"I'll miss him," Dad said.
"He's such a restful little fellow."

"He'll hate it there," Mom said.
"That family's always in such a rush.
They walk fast, drive fast, shop fast, and eat fast."

"Oh, Sloth will change all that," Amy said.

ART of PATIENCE
SLOW COOKING

And he did, very . . . very . . . slowly.